Crack Another Yolk

and other word play poems

Crack Another Yolk

AND OTHER WORD PLAY POEMS

COMPILED BY JOHN FOSTER

Illustrations by Clare Hemstock

Oxford University Press, Great Clarendon Street, Oxford OX2 6DP

Oxford New York
Auckland Bangkok Buenos Aires
Cape Town Chennai Dar es Salaam Delhi
Hong Kong Istanbul Karachi Kolkata Kuala Lumpur
Madrid Melbourne Mexico City Mumbai Nairobi
São Paulo Shanghai Taipei Tokyo Toronto

Oxford is a trade mark of Oxford University Press

First published 1996

A CIP catalogue record for this book is available from the British Library

ISBN 0 19 276098 X

7 9 10 8

Printed in China

Contents

An Angry Alligator

There's no such word as *allegate*,
But what am I to do?
An angry alligator
That I met at London Zoo
Is making allegations
That my theory is untrue.

Colin West

Propper English

Once upon a time I used
To mispell
To sometimes split infinitives
To get words of out order
To punctuate, badly
To confused my tenses
to ignore capitals
To employ 'common or garden' clichés
To exaggerate hundreds of times a day
But worst of all I used
To forget to finish what I

Alan F. G. Lewis

Allegate

Typewriting Class

Dear Miss Hinson
I am spitting
In front of my top ratter
With the rest of my commercesnail sturdy students
Triping you this later.
The truce is Miss Hinson
I am not hippy with my cross.
Every day on Woundsday
I sit in my dusk
with my type rutter
Trooping without lurking at the lattice
All sorts of weird messengers.
To give one exam pill,
'The quick down socks . . .
The quick brine pox . . .
The sick frown box . . .
The sick down jocks
Humps over the hazy bog'
When everyone kows
That a sick down jock
Would not be seen dead near a hazy bog.
Another one we tripe is;
'Now is the tame
For all guide men
To cram to the head
Of the pratty.'

To may why of sinking
I that is all you get to tripe
In true whelks of stirdy
Then I am thinking of changing
To crookery classes.
I would sooner end up a crook
Than a shirt hand trappist
Any die of the wink.
I have taken the tremble, Miss Hinson
To trip you this later
So that you will be able
To understand my indignation.
I must clothe now
As the Bill is groaning

Yours fitfully . . .

Gareth Owen

The Eraser Poem

The eraser poem.
The eraser poem
The eraser poe
The eraser po
The eraser p
The eraser
The erase
The eras
The era
The er
The e
The
Th
T

Louis Phillips

The , and the Full •

A sentence deep within a book
was causing quite a stir.
Before its full • could be reached
a problem would occur.

Despite a , in between
the readership would tend
to end up somewhat out of breath
before they reached the end.

Said the , to the full .
'All these words are packed too tight.
This sentence goes on far too long,
it isn't reading right.'

The full . bounced along the line,
inspecting every word.
'You're absolutely right,' he said,
'this passage is absurd!
The words will never disobey
the punctuation laws.
They know that I can make them stop,
while you just make them
pause.'

'We need more time,' the , said,
'but how can time be stolen?'
The full . hopped above his head
and made a ;

He stayed up there to chat a while;
the , found a friend.
The sentence read through perfectly,
at least until the end.

Jez Alborough

Spelling

If an **S** and an **I** and an **O** and a **U** with an **X** at the end spells Sioux,
And an **E** and a **Y** and an **E** spells eye—
Pray what is a speller to do?
If an **S** and an **I** and a **G** and an **H** and an **E** and a **D** spells sighed,
Pray what is there left for a speller to do but—
To go and commit Sioux-eye-sighed?

Anon

Spellbound

I have a spelling chequer
It came with my PC
It plainly marks four my revue
Miss takes I cannot sea.
I've run this poem threw it
I'm shore your pleased too no;
It's letter perfect in it's weigh
My chequer tolled me sew.

Norman Vandal

Life's a Spelling Test

Life's a spelling test
When I ask you, 'What's your name?'
For I may spell it differently,
Although it sounds the same.

Are you Catherine with a C,
Or Katherine with a K,
Or Kathryn with a y,
Or Catharine with an a?

Is it Stephen with ph
Or Steven with a v,
Are you Glenn with double n?
Do I spell Ann(e) with an e?

Are you Sophie with ie
Or Sophy with a y?
Are you Jon without an h
Or Clare without an i?

Life's a spelling test,
It's your parents who're to blame.
What's on your birth certificate
Is how *they* spelt your name.

John Foster

The Palindromes

Mr and Mrs Palindrome
Live in a house on a hill:
There's **Mum** and **Dad**
And **Nan** and **Bob**
And **Anna** and **Eve** and **Lil**.
There's **Otto** the dog
And **Pip** the **pup**—
Each has a funny name.
Spelt front to back
Or back to front
They come out just the same.

Eric Finney

Madam and Eve

There once was a fellow called Adam;
There once was a woman called Eve.
In the garden he said to her, *Madam,*
I'm Adam, or so I believe.
    Thus the very first word
    That our first mother heard
    In the ancestral home
    Was the first palindrome.
And the second was spoken to Adam,
When she with a smile replied, *Eve.*

Gerard Benson

Phoebus' Palindrome

I go down
As
Sun in evening
Drowning below world
Journeying with light
Into darkness:
Turning
Darkness into
Light, with journeying
World below, drowning
Evening in sun
As
Down go I.

Pam Gidney

An Acrostic

A favourite literary devi
Ce is the one whe
Re the first letter
Of each line spell
S out the subject the poe
T wishes to write about.
I must admit, I
Can't see the point myself.

Roger McGough

Brother

B ehaves like a maniac when grown-ups aren't watching

R ampages most when you want to be quiet

O rders you around as if you were his servant

T hinks endlessly of fresh ways to torment you

H ates above everything to hear you admired

E ats with loud noises simply to irritate

R esorts to being charming only as the last desperate bribe

Brian Merrick

Sister

S weet as syrup whenever it suits her
S our as old milk at all other times.
I s only good for messing things up, and
I nterfering where she's absolutely no business.
S hows no brains, wit, or humour but always
S impers like a moron when there's something she needs.
T eases and torments whenever you
T ry to concentrate.
E xasperates all of your friends with her
E xcrutiating charm and smarminess.
R educes anyone with sense to rage and frustration and is
R idiculously over-rated by everyone but me.

Brian Merrick

Riddle-Me-Right

Card magic is mighty easy to me, so are legerdemain and mesmerisM
Outlandish are my powers and my personality and my paraphernaliA
Nothing is to me impossible. No, nothing. Absolutely no thinG
Just try and explain my flashy, trashy, trumpery tricks. Try! I
Usually defy all measly, mundane explanations. Mysterious magiC
Rodomontade is my reason, my rhetoric, my rationale, my trade. I
Excel at deception, at disappearance, at inducing doubt. Am I A
Riddling mountebank, dear reader, or a miraculous master magiciaN

Gerard Benson

TALL STORY

Today, our teacher
Asked us to write
Lacrosse sticks in our English
Lesson. At least, that's what we thought

She said.
That's why most
Of us looked blank and
Replied, 'If it's all right with
You, we'd rather write high queues instead.'

John Foster

Nonsense Haiku

Flypaper

On the eight-ten train
Bluebottle reads the headlines,
The crossword complete.

Hairslide

The young bucks and does
Find nature's icy playground
And slip down, laughing.

Pillowcase

Sheets give evidence,
Duvet cover makes statement,
Bolster gets life term.

High Tea

On top of Snowdon
Golfers assemble, clubs drawn.
The match is begun.

Headrest

Half term holiday
Children, teachers, cleaners gone
Principal locks up.

Angi Holden

Code Haiku

23.8.1.20 1.18.5 20.8.5.19.5
14.21.13.2.5.18.19?
20.8.5.25 1.18.5 1. 13.5.19.19.1.7.5
9.14 3.15.4.5:
10.21.19.20 12.9.11.5 1. 16.15.5.13.

(for solution see p.94)

Dave Ward

Poem

A poem is like a step ladder
it sometimes seems to me

roof
the to
to make
up your
go point
You and

down again, stepping
carefully on each word.

Or occasionally it's
a strong tight rope
anchoring your thoughts to the deck poempoempoe
mpoempoempo
empoempoemp
oempoempoem

It can be as
short
or as long as the traditional piece of string.

A poem can do
its work for you
when it just

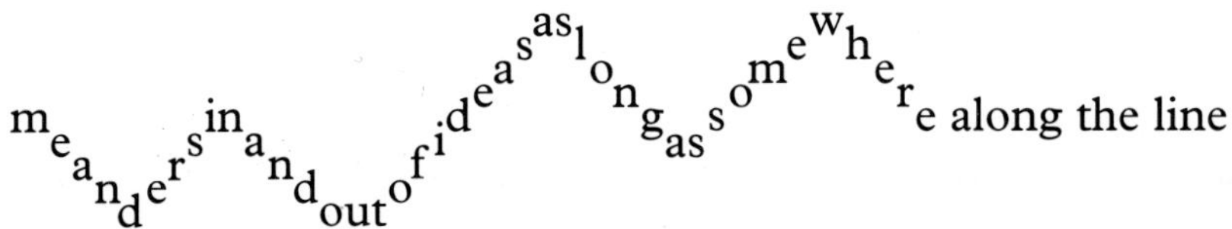
meanders in and out of ideas as long as somewhere along the line

it uses images and words
which are just right for
that poem and none other

words which belong behind and in front of one another
in an exact order and which could never play follow-my-leader
in any different poem

words
which
won't
f
a
l
l
o
f
f
at
the
END

Moira Andrew

Couplet

1
A couplet is two lines—two lines in rhyme.
The first comes easy, the second may take time.

2
Most couplets will have lines of equal length;
This gives them double dignity and strength.

3
Please count the syllables in 2 and say
How many. Ten each line? Correct! And they

4
In turn comprise the five-foot standard line:
Pentameter. The foot's *iambic*. Fine

5
Enough! On human feet, of course, our shoes
Do match; likewise the laces. If you choose

6
A briefer line,
Like this of mine,

7
Or say
OK.

8
Why, *these* are couplets, somewhat crude but true
To form. Try one yourself. See how you do.

9
Meanwhile, I'll give *you* one. Hand me that pen.
A four-foot line—eight syllables, not ten:

10
I cán / not síng / the óld / songs nów;
I név / er cóuld / sing án / y hów.

11
Couplets, you see, should make their stand alone.
I've used some differently, but that's my own

12
responsibility

David McCord

Silver

To find a rhyme for silver
Or any 'rhymeless' rhyme
Requires only will, ver-
bosity, and time.

Stephen Sondheim

Word Trap

'I've penned a poem,'
The poet cried.
The poem sighed,
Resting its word-weary head
Inside its cage
Of lines on the page
And waited to be read.

John Foster

Words in a Cage

The words in the cage
Made very small sounds
Pick Peck Tip Tap
Zip Zoo Seed Sad
Hip Hop and Hope

When they tried to move—
Flight Flutter Flagitate—
They flew into the bars
And just fell back.

One day we opened the cage
And they all flew out.
What a hullabaloo!
They exploded into song—
A carolling chorus:

Flamboyant Flamfleur!
Flavescent Flageolet!
Flawless Fluctuation!
Flarepath Flammation!

And as they all flew
Up into the sky
Their parting word
Fell about our ears:
Floccinaucinihilipilification!

Geoffrey Summerfield

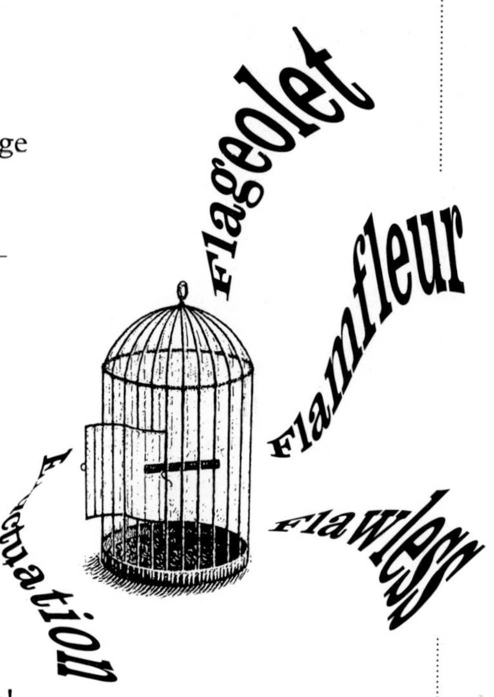

Words

A girl I know is fond of quick words, slick words,
Slip-out, shoot about, rapid fire, rat-a-tat-tat words—
Words like snick, splat, brunt, nimble, dodge, and zip.

The man across the road likes slow words, doughy words—
Earthbound, sludge-around, drawn-out, rambly words—
Words like puddle, bemoan, lonesome, cloudy, doze, and drizzle.

I have an uncle who prefers light words, bright words,
Float and fly, way-up high, airy-fairy, huff-puff words—
Words like jocular, bubble, whisper, disappear, magic, ping-pong.

A teacher at school uses weighty words, unmatey words,
Dark brown, hang-down, very serious, 'you will sit still' words—
Words like persevere, don't, punctual, never, behave, assessment.

I must say I am keen on savoursome words, flavoursome words,
Taste-bud tickling, tongue-trembling, delicious, nutritious words—
Words like gobstopper, crinkle chips, peanuts, and knickerbocker glory.

Jack Ousbey

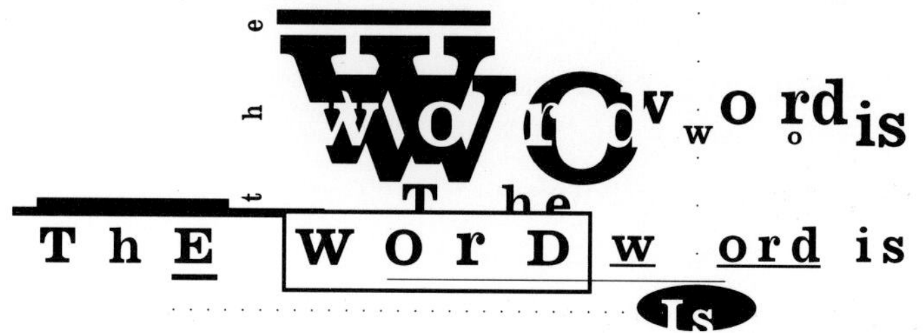

The Word Is

The word is:

you can eat them,
you can weigh them,
you can hang on them,
you can use one in jest,
you can pass one to the wise,
you can be as good as one,
you can place one in someone's ear,
you can take them right out of people's mouths,
you can lay down the law with one,
you can have the last and final one
and you can even be perfect with one.

But please don't take my word for it!

Ian Souter

A Begins Another

A is for 'ungry 'orses
B is for long
C is for sailing courses
D dum D D is for song.
E eeeee for a ghostly wail
F ort to be for work
G up said the horse on a mountain trail
H lost in honour found in house and puts the sh in shirk.
I is for you and me and one
J is for bird who chatters and squawks
K for Knight is there but dumb
L leads an 'ephant by the nose and is found in the middle of walks.
M is a W on stilts or the start of drawing a crown
N is the letter for 'velope
O is the sound of surprise written down
P is found in pod or tin or finishing the soap.
Q short or long it always waits
R RRR is a cheer of sorts
S is a snake and the sound that it makes
T is for shirt for leisure or sports.
U is not for you alone
V is a spear or an arrow head
W is not your twin
X marks the spot of treasure or wrong or a kiss to be read.
Y is a question asked many times over and over and over
Z and done is this alphabet
A begins another.

Julie Holder

A Hard Life Without Ease

Cook and wash and polish his boots,
Scrub that pot, scrub that pan,
Do that laundry, darn his socks,
Tidy round as fast as I can

And it's work, work, nothing but work!
Work is stuff
I just can't shirk,
I may stop but worlds will spin
So though I try, I just can't win!

Ploughing furrows, milking cows,
Oil that tractor, fix that pump,
Cutting corn and filling barns
Carting rubbish down that dump,

And it's work, work, nothing but work!
Work is stuff
I just can't shirk,
I may stop but worlds will spin,
So though I try, I just can't win!

Trying hard with long division,
Tidy writing all day long,
'List all products of Australia!'
Put my hand up, got it wrong.

And it's work, work, nothing but work!
Work is stuff
I just can't shirk,
I may stop but worlds will spin,
So though I try, I just can't win!

David Orme

Riddle

I am
word-cruncher,
wilful, square-brain,
a mind of my own;
I am words without end,
though silent as stone.
My head is a jumble
of poems not yet done;
a mumble of stories,
of number, of song.
I'm a dream-hoarder—
snatch my words,
catch if you can!
Snatch them and mix them,
make them your own!

Judith Nicholls

What Am I?

I'm never the same
from one minute
to the next.
In fiction writers flash
me in all directions
disrupting my flow
clocking up what
effect I have on
those who only know
part of my being.
I never stop
and am divided into
numbers and names
and sections. No one
really understands
how I tick.
Turn me round and you'll see
A widow's mite.
There is never enough of me
though I am ageless
Grandfathers speak loudly
Of my passing by.
I'm there in a way
In the song along with
Parsley, Sage, and Rosemary
The Ancient I am,
An Old father.

Sally Angell

(Solutions on p.94)

Who Are You?

my mum is your mum
my big sister
always goes around
with your big sister
when I kiss you
you kiss me
but when
I raise my right fist
to try and hit you
you catch it with your left
I can see you
but I'm never quite sure
if you can see me
I know
who I am
but
who knows
who you are
?

Dave Ward

abcdefGHIJKLMNOpqrst
UVWXYZABCDEFGHIJKLMNOpqrs
tuvWXYZABCDEFGHIJKLMNOPQRSTUVw
XYZABCDEFGHIJKLMNOPQRSTUVWXYZABC
DEFGHIJKLMNOPQRSTUVWXYZABCDEFGHIJK
MNOPQRSTUVWXYZABCDEFGHIJKLMNOPQRSTu
VWXYZABCDEFGHIjklmnopqrstuvwxyzabcdefghijklmnop
QRSTUVWXYZABCDEFGHIjklmnopqrstuvwxyzabcdefghijkl
MNOPQRSTUVWXYZABCDEFGHijklmnopqrstuvwxyzabcdefg
HIJKLMNOPQRSTUVWXYZABCDEFGhijklmnopqrstuvwxyzabcd
EFGHIJKLMNOPQRSTUVWXYZABCDEfghijklmnopqrstuvwxyzabc
DEFGHIJKLMNOPQRSTUVWXYZABCdefghijklmnopqrstuvwxyzabc
DEFGHIJKLMNOPQRSTUVWXYZABCDEFGHI jklmnopqrstuvwxyzab
CDEFGHIJKLMNOPQRSTUVWXYXABCEFGHIJklmnopqrstuvwxyzabc
DEFGHIJKLMNOPQRSTUVWXYZABCDEFghijklmnopqrstuvwxyzabcde
FGHIJKLMNOPQRSTUVWXYZABCDEFGHIJKlmnopqrstuvwxyzabcdef
GHIJKLMNOPQRSTUVWXYZABCDEFGHIJKlmnopqrstuvwxyzabcd
EFGHIJKLMNOPQRSTUVWXYZABCDabcdefghijklmnopqrstuvwXYZA
BCDEFGHIJKLMNOPQRSTUVwxyzabcdefghijklmnopqrstuvwxyzabcdefg
HIJKLMNOPQRSTUVWXYZABCDEFghijklmNOPQRSTuvwxyzabcdefghij
KLMNOPQRSTUVWXYZabcdefghIJKLMNOPQRSTuvwxyzabcdefghijklmnop
QRSTUVWXYZABCCEFGHIJKLMNOPQRSTUVWXYabcdefghijklmnopqrst
UVWXYZABCDEFGHIJKLmnopQQRSTUVWXYzabcdefghijklmnopqrstuvw
XYZABCDEFGHIJKLMNopqrstuvwxYZABCDEFGHijklmnopqrstuvwxy
ZABCDEFGHIJKLMNOpqrstuvwXYZABCDEFGHIJKLMnopqrstuvw
XYZABCDEFGHIJKLMOPqrstuvwXYZABCdefghijklmnopqrstuvwxyz
ABCDEFGHIJKLMNOPQRSTUVWXYZabcdefghiJKLMNOPQRSt
UVWXYZABCDEFGHIJKLMNOPQRstuvwxABCdefghijkLMNO
PQRSTUVWXYZABCDEFGHIJKLMNopqrSTUvwxYZABCDE
FGHIJKLMNOPQRSTUVWXYZabcdefGHIJKlmnopqrstuv
WXYZABCDEFGHIJKLMNopQRStuvwxyzabcdefghijk
LMNOPQRSTUVWXYZAbcDEfghijklmnopqrstu
VWXYZABCDEFGHIJKLMNopqrstuvwxyza
ABCDEFGHIJKLMNOPQRStuvwxyzabcd
EFGHIJKLMNOPQRSTUVwxyzabcdef
GHIJKLMNOPQRSTUVWXyzabcdef
GHIJKLMNOPQRSTUV
WXYZABCDEF
GHIJKLMNO
PQRSTUV
WXYZA
BCD
EF

1234567890!@£$%^&*
1234567890!@£$%^&*012
4567890!@£$%^&*012345678
0!@£$%^&*01234567890!@£$%
^&*01234567890!@£$%^&*012
34567890!@£$%^&*0123456789
0!@£$%^&*01234567890!@£$%
^&*01234567890!@£$%^&*0123
4567890!@£$%^&*01234567890
!@£$%^&*01234567890!@£$
%^&*01234567890!@£$%^&
^&01234567890!@£$%^
*01234567890!@
&*012345
£$%^&*01234567
^&*012345
890!@£$%
^&*012
3456
78

Two Riddles

It's what happens after
The goodbyes have been said;
Or perhaps it's a track
Through what covers your head.

You're Emperor, Conqueror, King,
You dead straight thing.

Eric Finney

(Solutions on p.94)

Anagriddles

In each verse, the words in heavy type are an anagram of the word which is the answer to the riddle. The solutions can be found on p.94.

This might have helped
To avoid the woe
Of aching teeth
That **both hurt so**.

We find in the universe
Much to amaze us.
We study the heavens:
Moon-starers, star-gazers.

It makes **mouths ace**
On many a fellow's face.

In a café she'll produce a
Meal: lunch, tea or supper.
She might offer you, '**A stew, sir?**'
Or maybe just a cuppa.

Boy friend, girl friend,
True-love, dear:
There we sat
Fair words to hear.

Penalty for crime—
Let's make it tough:
I'd say **nine thumps**
Might be enough.

Eric Finney

The Name of the Game

Play with names
And Pat becomes tap.
Karl is a lark
And Pam is a map.

Miles is slime.
Liam is mail.
Bart is a brat.
Lina's a nail.

Stan tans.
Gary turns gray.
Norma's a Roman.
Amy makes May.

Tabitha's habitat.
Leon is lone.
Kate is teak.
Mona's a moan.

Trish is a shirt.
Kay is a yak.
But whatever you do,
Jack remains Jack.

John Foster

Word Puzzle

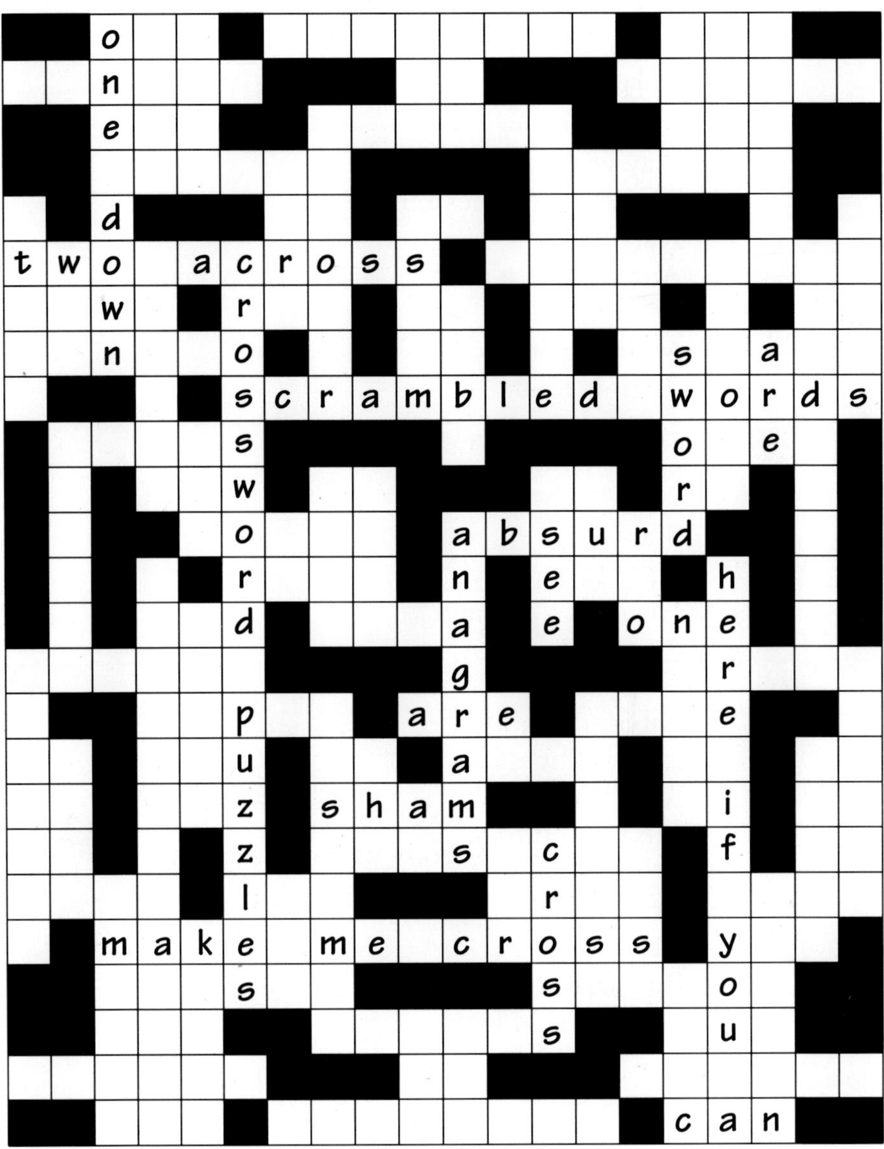

Margaret Blount

It Takes One To Know One

LIBRARIANS take it as read
HISTORIANS take you aback
CARPENTERS take the edge off
REBELS take up cudgels
HOROLOGISTS take one's time
CARDIOLOGISTS take heart
TAXI DRIVERS take you for a ride
SNOOKER PLAYERS take one's cue
KLEPTOMANIACS take it from there
PILOTS take off
PATIENTS take their medicine
HURDLERS take a running jump
COSMETICIANS take a powder
SURGEONS take it out of you
SOLDIERS take steps
DUELLISTS take the point
PURSUERS take after me
HYPOCRITES take on the appearance of
GOOD SAMARITANS take somebody in
LEVITATORS take somebody up on something
WASHERWOMEN take down a peg or two
FOOTBALL MANAGERS take somebody on one side
EXECUTIONERS take something to one's head

BUT ME . . . I can take it or leave it!

Gervase Phinn

Doctor Spooner's Country Walk

It was roaring with pain
As he load down the strain
With his holly over his bread.
Dunce every way
He would wavel that tray
Sometime between buncheon and led.

He popped near a stark
With the sky dearly nark
Although it was diddle of May.
The church rock was clinging,
A sobin was ringing
In a sky that was groudy and clay.

He palled at a cub
For a grat and some chub
And a serving of good wed and brine.
Then, lack in the bane
In right of the Spain
He thought the fawning was mine.

But ten it was woo
He turned his vac on the bue
As he wanted to be weir his knife
He'd been out for who towers
So he flicked her some powers
As he needed no stubble and trife.

Then strengthening his lied
To be there sigh her bide
He suddenly stripped on a tone.
And haking his shed,
The sore old pole said,
'I'm hurt and I'm ear on my hone!'

His wife, Jady Lane
Came quick lown the dane
And saw that her starling had dumbled.
'Oh! you door pier,
Let's get home, it's night queer;'
He rose and growfully wumbled—

'I've hanged my bed,
My blows has just ned
And in my pest there's a chain.
I've shut my kin
And chumped my bin
So forgive me for
pouring with rain . . .'

David Whitehead

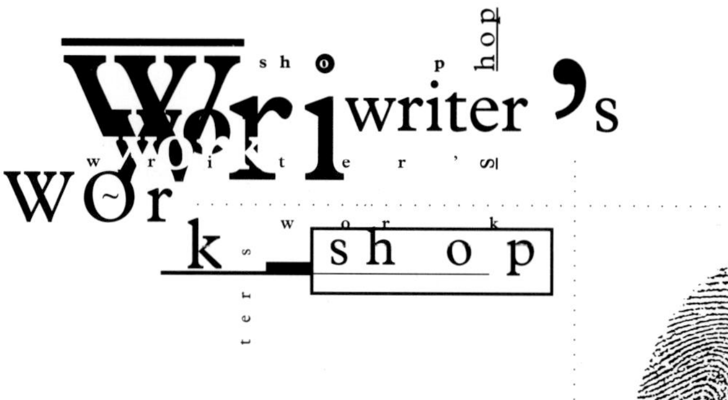

Writer's Workshop

A scribble of writers scrabbling for new ways,
Crossing out and changing, making blots of mistakes.
Herd of oxymoron in the background, brightly snoring,
A litter of alliteration on the look out, lying low,
A chorus could come in, chanting, chanting,
A repeated refrain here and there, here and there,
Metaphors are matadors, they add their flourishes,
Similes wait like actors in the wings.
A scribble of writers now searching for an ending.
A question? Or a shock! Or a gentle fade . . .
Reach for the tools to hammer out those sentences.
A workshop of writing waiting to be made.

Michaela Morgan

A Fistful of Pacifists

A thimbleful of giants
A rugby scrum of nuns
An atom of elephants
A cuddle of guns

A rustle of rhinoceros
A barrel of bears
A swear box of politicians
A bald patch of hairs

A stumble of ballet dancers
A flutter of whales
A mouthful of silence
A whisper of gales

A pocketful of earthquakes
A conference of pears
A fistful of pacifists
A round-up of squares

David Kitchen

N.U.P. Report

The National Union
of Peacemakers
held
their annual conference
at Peacehaven.

Delegates arrived
from Concord, Massachusetts,
but
none was invited
from Wargrave or Warminster.

During the teabreak
they played
'Kiss
In The Ring'.
War Games were vetoed.

A peaceful day
was enjoyed by
all,
and nobody gave anybody
a peace of their mind.

Polly Sinclair

Crack Another Yolk

At breakfast we scramble to sit
and egg each other on,
cracking yolk after yolk.
To my sister I say, 'You're chicken.'
She says, 'You've an addled head.'
'Look at the sun. He side up,' I say.
'It's enough to make you turn white,' she replies.
'That's a fowl yolk,' I cry,
'and it's one you've poached from me.'
She says, 'You're not eggs actly right.
If you see a leg, then pullet.'

Our mum's become hardboiled to this.
She takes it all with a pinch of salt.

Barrie Wade

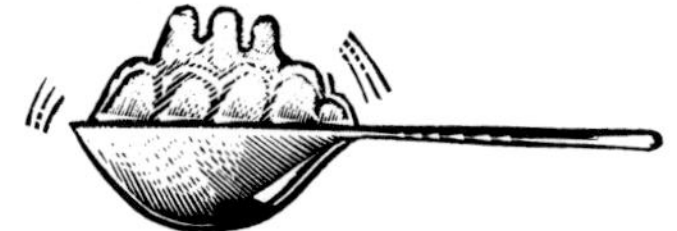

Jelly and Melons

When Jilly eats jelly,
Then Jilly is jolly.
But melons make Melanie
Most melancholy.

Colin West

Slimming

I want to be a Rake
But
I want another bit of Cake.
Why
Can't I have my Cake
And
Eat it?

Sally Crabtree

Eataweek

Bunsday
Stewsday
Henseggday
Burgerday
Pieday
Spaghettiday
Sundae.

John Coldwell

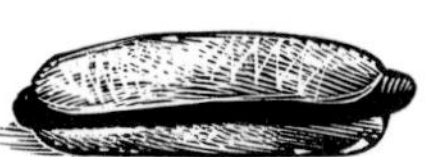

Dorothy Hogg had a hot dog stand:
Hottest dogs in all the land.
East and south and north and west
Dot Hogg's hot dogs were the best!

Kit Wright

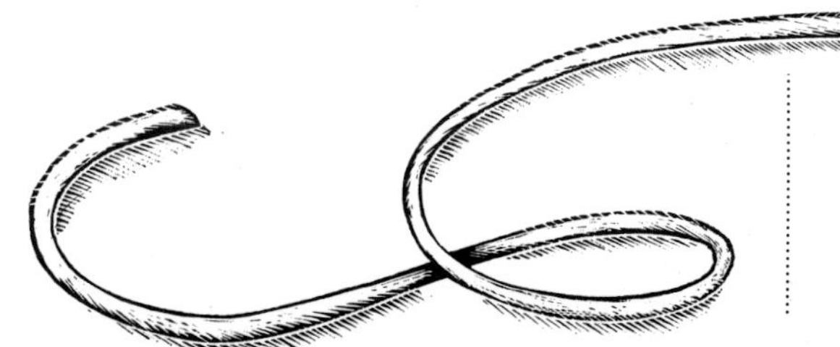

Trousers is a Silly Name

Like scissors:
A silly things
They is.
Always talking
Like there's
Two of it—
Or more!
(And flies . . .
Who thought up
That . . . or those?!)
I'm off to put on
  my new trouser;
Or shall I wear
  my jean?
  my short?
  my trunk?
The fact that I've
  two legs
  are no excuses;
I've got
  two arm
But I don't put on
  my shirts
  each days.

Trousers is
A silly name.
But we call our dog it
Just the same.
Is that why he eats
Enough for two??

Trevor Millum

An Odd Kettle of Fish

The detectives said that
the books had been cooked.
(They tasted good.)

My teacher said we could
have a free hand.
(I added it to my collection.)

Some people bottle up
their feelings.
(I keep mine in a jar.)

My mother said—
'Hold your tongue!'
(It was too slippery.)

When my sister laughs
she drives me round the bend.
(I catch the bus back.)

Dad told me
to keep a stiff upper lip.
(It's in a box by my bed.)

My uncle is a terrible
name dropper.
(I help my aunt
to sweep them up.)

In the school races
I licked everyone in the class.
(It made my tongue sore.)

Pie Corbett

Rhyme-osaur

Out of a deep, dark mine-osaur
at roughly half past nine-osaur,
emerged a drowsy stegosaur
into the warm sunshine-osaur.
He warmed his chilly spine-osaur
which made him feel divine-osaur.

He nibbled on a pine-osaur
and drank a glass of wine-osaur,
but then he saw a sign-osaur
which made him yelp and whine-osaur.
It forecast his decline-osaur,
his time had come to die-nosaur!

John Rice

Incident

A dinosaur
caught his feet in a door

and then he was
a dino-SORE.

Iain Crichton Smith

Terrible Lizard

My first is in teeth and also in tum.
My second is in tasty and also in yum.
My third is in hunger but not in food.
My fourth is in apples but not in chewed.
My fifth is in nice and also in naughty
My sixth is in one but never in forty.
My seventh is in onions but not in chalk.
My eighth is in steak but not on a fork.
My ninth is in meat but not in cheese
My tenth is in custard but not in please.
My eleventh is in pears but not in peaches
My twelfth is in puddle but not on beaches.
My thirteenth is in scatter but not in come
My fourteenth is in danger so don't act dumb
My fifteenth is in eating and also in ate.
My sixteenth is in taxi so you won't be late.
For I am the king of a terrible breed.
Come too close and I'll have a jolly good feed.

Janis Priestley

Tyrannosaurus Rex

Stanley Cook

Can You?

Can you cross the bridge in your nose
and run between the gap in your teeth
to mend the roof in your mouth
with the nails in your toes?
No!
Well why not climb the palm in your hand
and watch out for the swallow in your throat.
Or,
just get up early one morning instead
and catch the hares asleep on your head!

Ian Souter

The Whether Forecast

'This is the Whether Forecast.
I don't know whether it will rain or not.'

Leo Aylen

The New Weatherperson's First Appearance

Here is the blether warcast
for Flyday the dirty-worst
of Knockedover:
    This week's cold smell
    will get curse
    towards frightfall
    with wail-force winds
    and freezing frog.
    Watch out for black lice on the toads.

Ian Serraillier

You Tell Me

Here are the football results:
League Division Fun
Manchester United won, Manchester City lost.
Crystal Palace 2 Buckingham Palace 1
Millwall Leeds nowhere
Wolves 8 A cheese roll and had a cup of tea 2
Aldershot 3, Buffalo Bill shot 2
Evertonil, Liverpool's not very well either
Newcastle's Heaven, Sunderland's a very nice place 2
Ipswhich one? You tell me.

Michael Rosen

Dennis Madge*

Choir peas!
Love nifty
Love Bertie
Canteen dirty
Dirty overall
Dirty daughter
Juice!
Aunty Madge Pat
Game
Pat bleeds Sam by
too sex to love

*or, it's not what you serve
it's the way that you spin it

Trevor Millum

Passers-by

A passer-by
Was passing by
A bypass,
And passing by
The bypass,
A passer-by
Passed by;
By passing by
A bypass
As a passer-by
Passed by,

A passer-by
Was passed by
By a bypass
Passer-by.

Colin West

Baby Driver

I'd like to drive a tractor
  or maybe even a bus,
my mother says I drive her crazy
  by creating so much fuss.

I'd drive my brand new Honda
  do wheelies, skids and swerves,
I drive my father round the bend
  by getting on his nerves.

I'd like to drive at Brands Hatch
  and be part of the Grand Prix action,
my sister says I'm very good
  at driving people to distraction.

A driver's life is very hard
  you have to be tough and brave,
my family say that very soon
  I shall drive them to the grave!

John Rice

Life of the Nation

Delivered in Bournemouth,
Walked in Stepney,
Talked in Chatham,
Educated in Reading and Countam,
Laboured in Workington,
Married in Weddington,
Raised family in Kidderminster,
Retired to Lazenby,
Slight pain in Akenham,
Felt worse in Sickinghall,
Recovered in Welling,
Relapsed in Illingworth,
Died in Paston,

Laid to rest in Bury.

John Coldwell

Epitaphs

Magistrate

Here lies an honest magistrate
Corrupt and dissolute of late

Sculptor

A sculptor cunning in art
Could life to bronze impart
Cast in heroic mould
Now lies cold

Shy Man

Here lie I
No longer shy
So come on Miss
Give us a kiss

Sudden Death

How I went I'll never know
I didn't stay to see me go

On the tombstone of a man who passed away just as he was lighting his favourite pipe

Puffed it 'n' snuffed it

Socialite

A prominent socialite
Knew every leading light
Save death
Whom she met
One party night

Baker

A baker here forever lies
Fell in an oven and failed to rise

Cow

It's not much fun
Knowing one day
I could be
Very well done

Hare

Here lies a hare
Come to a split end

Jack

Here lies Jack
Asleep in his box

Curtain

Here lies a curtain
Hung
Drawn
And quartered

Peter Bennett

Dodo

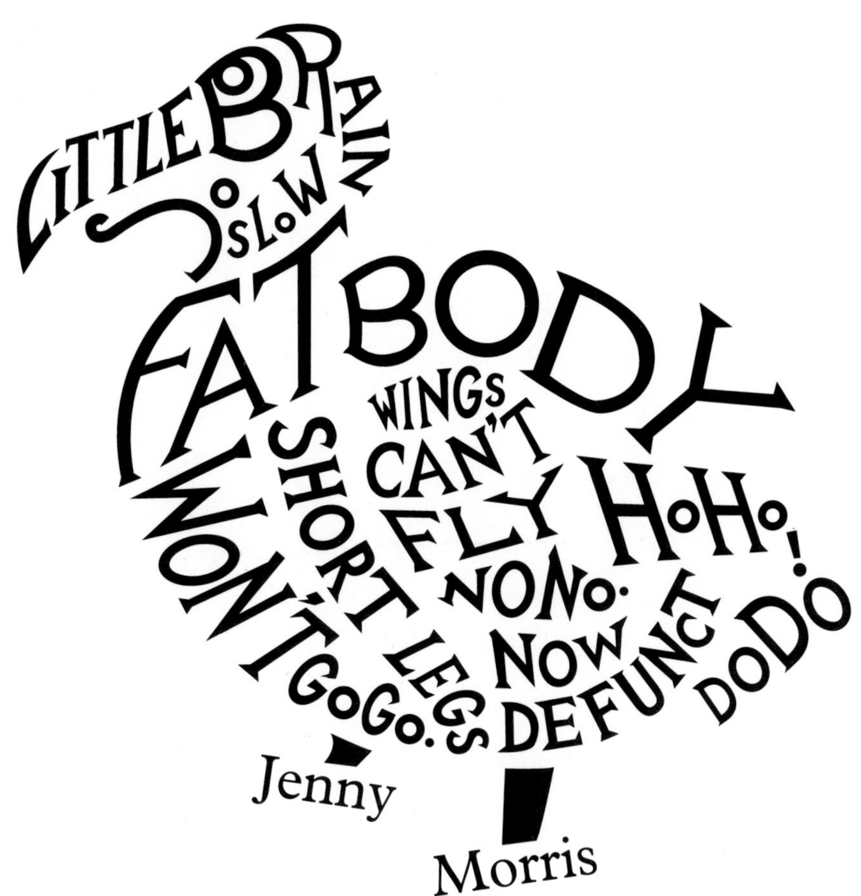

Jenny Morris

The Praying Mantis

The praying mantis seems to be
Intent on its devotions,
And yet its intellect is free
Of all religious notions.

The mantis male thinks, in a daze
Of love, 'I'll court and win her!'
But when he has, the female preys.
She snaps him up for dinner.

Dick King-Smith

A Yak from the Hills of Iraq

A yak from the hills of Iraq
Met a yak he had known awhile back.
    They went out to dine,
    And talked of lang syne—
Yak-ety, yak-ety, yak.

Willard R. Espy

The New Gnus

A gnu who was new to the zoo
Asked another gnu what he should do.
The other gnu said, shaking his head,
If I knew, I'd tell you, I'm new too.

John Foster

The Ptarmigan

The ptarmigan is strange
As strange as he can be;
Never sits on ptelephone poles
Or roosts upon a ptree.
And the way he ptakes to spelling
Is the strangest thing pto me.

Anon

How to Tell a Camel

The **D**romedary has one hump,

The **B**actrian has two.
It's easy to forget this rule,
So here is what to do.
Roll the first initial over
On its flat behind:

The **B**actrian is different from

The **D**romedary kind.

J. Patrick Lewis

A Flamingo

A Flamingo
is
a
long
cooooooooool
drink
of
something
pink

J. Patrick Lewis

Leopard

The leopard is a crafty cat
His camouflage is dotted
He hides among the dappled leaves
Yet, even then he's spotted.

David Whitehead

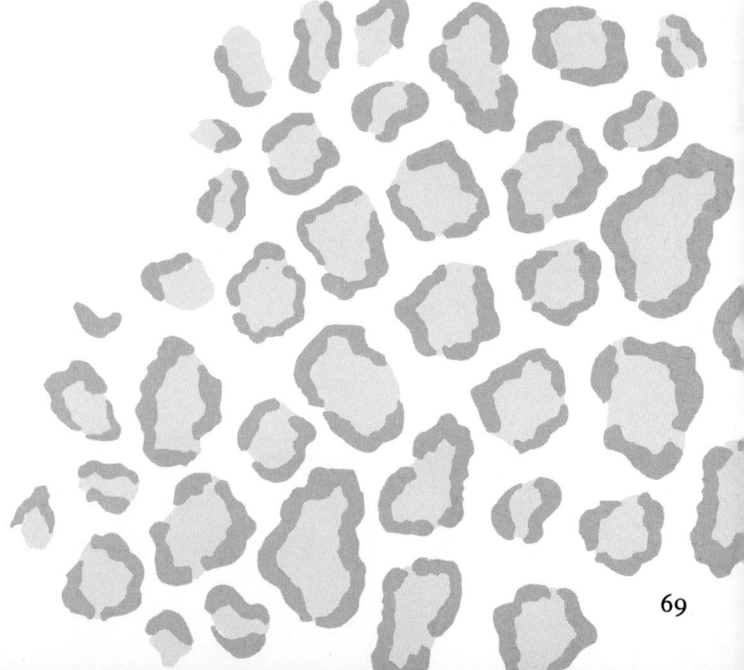

Ten Things You Probably Never Thought To Ask About Elephants

1. What do elephants say when they meet each other?
   'ELlo.
2. How do elephants choose their leaders?
   By ELEction.
3. How do elephants contact distant relatives?
   By ELEPHone.
4. What do elephants like best at the fairground?
   The 'ELter skELter.
5. How do elephants get upstairs?
   They take the ELEvator.
6. How do elephants improve their speech?
   They take ELocution lessons.
7. How do young elephants get married?
   They ELope.
8. What do old elephants take to grow young again?
   ELixir.
9. What do elephants shout when they're in danger?
   'ELp!
10. What do most elephants do in the evening?
    Watch ELEvision.

Tony Mitton

Someone Stole The

While I was taking a short   -nap
someone stole the   ,
I should have spun round like a   herine wheel
when someone stole the   .
But I was too slow to   ch them,
when someome stole the   .

Now the   amaran can't float,
because someone stole the   .
And the   erpillar can't crawl,
because someone stole the   .
And the   aract can't fall,
because someone stole the   .

It was not me and it was not you
but it is   egorically true,
And if you were to ask me
I'd say it was a   astrophe
That someone's stolen the   .

Brian Patten

MY SNAKE

My snake, a long and limber pet,
is practising the alphabet,
he demonstrates immense finesse
in shaping a curvaceous S.
He follows his initial show
by closing up into an O,
then fabricates an F and G
with enviable artistry.

My snake, with neither pad nor pen,
delineates a splendid N,
an agile W, a supple L,
an X with little parallel,
a shapely J, a graceful A,
a seamless C, a clever K,
then pausing for a breath or two,
he turns himself into a U.

My snake, with every skilful twist,
appends a letter to his list,
he makes an E, he forms an M,
a Y and V come after them,
he diagrams a dextrous D,
a subtle T, a nimble Z,
a convoluted curly Q,
a virtuoso W.

My snake, performing like a star,
portrays a P, enacts an R,
contorts into a brilliant B
with stylish sinuosity.
And yet, though he may stretch and shake,
one single point eludes my snake,
despite his most ingenious try,
he simply cannot dot his I.

Jack Prelutsky

Saints

St Ocking is the saint for socks
St Ar for the deep black night
St Icking Plaster for after shocks
St Ew for a tough old bite

St Ickleback's the man for stings,
St Alagmite for drips,
St Amp for postage, sending things,
St Eak goes well with chips.

Who's your particular favourite one?
St Egosaur for dunces?
St Itch for what you get at a run?
St Ick 'Em Up as the man with the gun says?

St Ick is the holy man for glue—
Or, on his day off, for hockey—
The naming of the saints is over to you;
St Ink!
St Ingy!
St Ocky!

Candia McWilliam

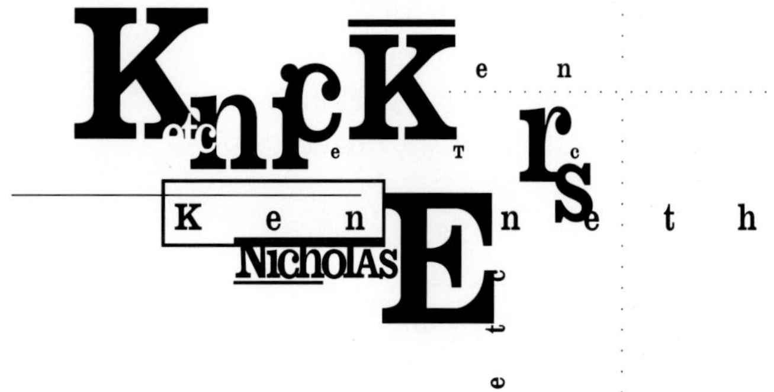

Kenneth Nicholas, Etc.

Kenneth Nicholas Ian Christopher
Keith Emmanuel Reginald Stoneley
Decided his name was too much of a mouthful,
So now he signs by initials only.

Wendy Cole

At the End of School Assembly

Miss Sparrow's lot flew out,
Mrs Steed's lot galloped out,
Mr Bull's lot got herded out,
Mrs Bumble's lot buzzed off.

Miss Rose's class . . . rose,
Mr Beetle's class . . . beetled off,
Miss Storm's class thundered out,
Mrs Frisby's class whirled across the hall.

Mr Train's lot made tracks,
Miss Ferry's lot sailed off,
Mr Roller's lot got their skates on,
Mrs Street's lot got stuck halfway across.

Mr Idle's class just couldn't be bothered,
Mrs Barrow's class were wheeled out,
Miss Stretcher's class were carried out
And
Mrs Brook's class
Simply
t r i c k l e d
a
w
a
y

Simon Pitt

Maths is Dangerous—
The Diary of an Accident Prone Mathematician

Monday
Run down by a protractor.

Tuesday
Fell out of a geometry.

Wednesday
Nearly drowned myself indices.

Thursday
Cut myself on the axis of symmetry.

Friday
Banged my head on multiplication table.

Nothing seems to add up any more.
My brain is getting number and number . . .

John Coldwell

Watch

1 is a left-handed arrow.
2 is kneeling in prayer.
3 is two bites out of 8.
4 is a nose with one hair.
5 is the stroke of a swimmer.
6 is a trampoline tuck.
7's a corner collapsing.
8's knot got an end—have a look.
9 is a tear with a tail to tell that
10U £10.
11's a 2 to a Roman.
12's *'want to'* when counting sounds.

Gina Douthwaite

Counting Them Out

One's a singular sort of chap.
One stands alone. One knows one's place.
Two's a hypocrite with more than one face.
Three's a hat-trick punching the air.
Four's solid and strong. Four stands square.
Five is moody: a handshake or a fist.
Six's knickers are in a twist.
Is she six of one or half a dozen of the other?
Seven is wicked—the deadly sins.
Eight's a miser who grins with pleasure,
As he gloatingly counts his pieces of treasure.
Nine is a person who's had one too many.
Ten's a common lot you can get for a penny.

John Foster

Bun Stew . . .

Bun
Stew
I've lost a shoe
Free
Floor
Ain't got no more
Dive
Snicks
I'm in a fix
Threading
Date
I'm gonna be late
Mine
Den
Ain't seen both shoes
Since I don't know when
Elephant
Shelve
I've dug all the cupboards
So now I'll delve
Shirtbean
Shortbean
It ain't where it ought been
Fistbean
Snicksbean
Gotta be quicksbean
Threadingbean
Datebean
Time don't waitbean
Minebean
Plenty
Just have to hop
With one foot empty . . .

Julie Holder

The Mad Parrot's Countdown

10 9 Wait (!)
Pieces of 8 pieces of 8
TERMINATE
7 6 Are you still alive
My hearties? 5
Gold rings but listen I've
Learnt more
4
(Make Love not War)
3 2
It's down to you
Yo ho ho Yo ho WHO (?)
1
Is 1
Is a bottle of rum
And ever more shall be so
Be so be so
Be Z E R 0 . . .

John Mole

Weight and Measure

Can you guess the weight of a wish?
An ounce away from a million ifs.

Can you guess the length of laughter?
Sixty-six golden chains without end.

Can you guess how heavy is 'I want'?
About a thousand tons of 'you can't have'.

Can you guess the metres in happiness?
Same as a butterfly or whale's breath.

Do you know the height of friendship?
Pace out the sky then double it.

Do you know the depth of fun?
Between a thimbleful and ocean.

Do you know how high is good?
Look around and up and down.

Do you know how many litres in love?
Silly question, litres measure liquid.

John Fairfax

To MLE

O, MLE, what XTC
I MN8 when UIC!
I used to rave of LN's II,
4 LC I gave countless sighs;
4 KT, and for LNR
I was a keen competitor;
But each now's a non-NTT,
4 UXL them all UC.

Louise J. Walker

40-love

middle aged
couple playing
ten- nis
when the
game ends
and they
go home
the net
will still
be be-
tween them

Roger McGough

Out of Joint

Mum ran off with the butcher,
she gave my dad the chop
and now they very rarely meet
unless it's in the shop.

Gina Douthwaite

A Dentist Named Archibald Moss

A dentist named Archibald Moss
Fell in love with the dainty Miss Ross.
Since he held in abhorrence
Her Christian name, Florence,
He renamed her his dear dental Floss.

Anon

Charles Dickens Caught the Devil

Charles Dickens caught the devil
Stealing Charles Dickens's chickens!
'What the dickens?' cried the devil.
'What the devil?' cried Charles Dickens.

Willard R. Espy

A Gottle o' Geer

When the ventriloquist lost his dummy
On a train that was bound for Wales,
He tried to give vent to his feelings
By throwing his voice on the rails.

But it killed his act completely . . .

Trevor Harvey

Count Dracula's Castle Hotel

**(Come for the weekend—risk staying for ever!
Exceptional Night Service—well stocked cellar.)**

VISITOR'S BOOK

Please sign the book
Upon the table
Before you leave
(If you feel able)

NAME	ADDRESS	COMMENTS
The Tooth Fairy	Finder Place, Userley-Under-The-Pillow	A **very** quiet weekend indeed . . .
The Sleeping Beauty	***Spellbinders Palace***	***Prick my finger—see me bleed!***
The Invisible Man	*Clearview-by-the-Sea*	*Uninterrupted sleep all night!*
Frankenstein	**Tin Creak, Oilando**	**I'm NUTS about this place— all right?**
The Famous Five	At the Smugglers' Cave, Through the Secret Passage, By the Hangman's Grave	SUPER feasts at midnight! (Golly!) Tim LOVED the bones— and the bat was jolly tasty, too . . . Must see the Count before we leave To thank him for the steaks we've found— But though we've hunted high and low He doesn't seem to be around. Gosh. Sorry. Must fly. 'Bye! SU - PER!

Trevor Harvey

Ghost

I
t
s
o t o
d
t
h
e
r
s m r a s t i h t o b g n i s i a r a i s i n g b o t h i t s a r m s
u
e
f
u
l
l
y
a
n
d
v
e
r
y
g r a d u a l l y d i s a p p e a r e d

Raymond Wilson

Kite

I'm
part of a
project on flight.
I'm supposed to attain
a great height. But
unfortunately
I got stuck
in a tree
so
it
looks
like
I'm
here
for
the
night!

June Crebbin

Sea's Cape

I
see
gulls
Icy
gulls
I see
gulls screaming
—Aye—
I see seagulls
screaming, see
Ai YUY—
scream

. . . 'Ice *ÇREAM*'
the seagulls
seem to scream
Hi Hi *eee*
Ye—Icy seagulls

I see

Gulls see

eyes

cream

Michael Horovitz

Miniskirt

miniskirtminiskirt
miniskirtminiskirtmi
niskirtminiskirtminisk
irtminiskirtminiskirtmin
legleglegleglegleglegleglegleg legleglegleglegleglegleglegleg
shoe shoe

Anthony Mundy

Chilly

I'm ch-ch-ch-ch-ch-ch-ch-ch-chilly,
I'm c-c-c-c-c-c-c-c-cold,
I was s-s-s-s-s-s-s-s-silly,
Should have worn my c-c-coat like I was told,
Now I'm s-s-s-s-s-s-s-s-sorry,
Cos I th-th-th-th-think I'm going to freeze,
Let me in! Can I sit and warm up a little bit,
P-p-p-p-p-p-p-p-p-p-PLEASE?

Now it's s-s-s-s-s-s-s-s-snowing,
And my b-b-b-b-body's losing heat,
My poor nose is g-g-g-g-g-g-glowing,
And I've lost the f-f-feeling in my feet,
How my teeth are ch-ch-ch-ch-ch-ch-chattering,
And I think I'm going to s-s-s-s-sneeze,
Let me in! Can I sit and warm up a little bit,
P-p-p-p-p-p-p-p-p-p-PLEASE?

Kaye Umansky

Freeze

The windowsill has grown a beard

c c
i i
c c
l l
e e

Milk bottles raise their caps
While puddles crack like broken glass

And trees wear furry wraps.

Susan Cowling

End Games

loose ends
split ends
dead ends
means and ends
end over
end up
fag ends
tail ends
butt ends
end of time
end of the line
endless
endings

the end

Katie Campbell

Answers

Code Haiku (p.23)
What are these numbers?
They are a message in code:
just like a poem.
The code is simple:
A=1
B=2 . . . etc.

Riddle (p.34)
Word-processor

What am I? (p.35)
Time

Who Are You? (p.36)
A reflection in a mirror

Two Riddles (p.37)
1. Parting
2. Ruler

Anagriddles (p.38)
1. Toothbrush
2. Astronomers
3. Moustache
4. Waitress
5. Sweetheart
6. Punishment

Acknowledgements

The Editor and publisher are grateful to the following for permission to include poems: **Moira Andrew**: for 'Poem', Copyright © Moira Andrew 1987, from Moira Andrew (ed): *Go and Open the Door* (Macmillan, 1987). **Sally Angell**: for 'What Am I?', Copyright © Sally Angell 1966, first published here. **Leo Aylen**: for 'The Whether Forecast', Copyright © Leo Aylen 1991. **Peter Bennett**: for 'Epitaphs', Copyright © Peter Bennett 1996, first published here. **Gerard Benson**: for 'Riddle-me-Right', Copyright © Gerard Benson 1978, from *Strolling Players* (Evans, 1978); and for 'Madam and Eve', Copyright © Gerard Benson 1981, first published in *New Statesman*, 1981. **Margaret Blount**: for 'Word Puzzle', Copyright © Margaret Blount 1996, first published here. **Katie Campbell**: for 'End Games', Copyright © Katie Campbell 1996, first published here. **Cassell plc**: for 'The Praying Mantis' by Dick King-Smith from *Alphabeasts* (Victor Gollancz Ltd). **John Coldwell**: for 'Eataweek' and 'Maths is Dangerous—the Diary of an Accident Prone Mathematician', Copyright © John Coldwell 1996, first published here; and for 'Life of the Nation', Copyright © John Coldwell 1992 from *The Slack-Jawed Camel* (Stride, 1992). **Wendy Cole**: for 'Kenneth Nicholas, Etc.' Copyright © Wendy Cole 1996, first published here. **Pie Corbett**: for 'An Odd Kettle of Fish', Copyright © Pie Corbett 1996, first published here. **Susan Cowling**: for 'Freeze', Copyright © Susan Cowling 1989, first published in Wes Magee (ed): *Madtail, Miniwhale* (Viking Kestrel, 1989). **Sally Crabtree**: for 'Slimming', Copyright © Sally Crabtree 1996, first published here. **Jennifer Curry**: for 'N.U.P. Report' by Polly Sinclair, Copyright © Jennifer Curry 1992, from Jennifer Curry (ed): *Dove on the Roof*, (Methuen Children's Books, 1992). **Gina Douthwaite**: for 'Out of Joint', Copyright © Gina Douthwaite 1996, first published here; and for 'Watch' from *Picture a Poem*, Copyright © Gina Douthwaite 1994 (Random House Children's Books). **Willard R. Espy**: for 'A Yak from the Hills of Iraq', and 'Charles Dickens Caught the Devil', Copyright © Willard R. Espy 1996, first published here. **John Fairfax**: for 'Weight and Measure', Copyright © John Fairfax 1996, first published here. **Eric Finney**: for 'The Palindromes', 'Two Riddles' and 'Anagriddles', Copyright © Eric Finney 1996, first published here. **John Foster**: for 'The Name of the Game', 'Word Trap' and 'Counting Them Out', all Copyright © John Foster 1996, first published here; 'Life's a Spelling Test' and 'Tall Story' from *Standing on the Sidelines* (OUP, 1995), Copyright © John Foster 1995; and 'The New Gnus' from *Four O'Clock Friday* and Other Poems (OUP, 1991), Copyright © John Foster 1991. **Pam Gidney**: for 'Phoebus' Palindrome', Copyright © Pam Gidney 1987, first published in Moira Andrews (ed): *The Unicorn and Lions* (Macmillan, 1987). **HarperCollins Publishers Limited**: for 'Typewriting Class' by Gareth Owen from *Song of the City*, (Young Lions, 1985), Copyright © Gareth Owen 1985. **George G Harrap & Co Ltd**: for 'Couplet', lines from 'Write me a Verse' by David McCord from *Mr Bidery's Spidery Garden* (1972). **Trevor Harvey**: for 'Count Dracula's Castle Hotel' and 'A Gottle o' Geer', Copyright © Trevor Harvey 1996, first published here. **Angi Holden**: for 5 'Nonsense Haiku', Copyright © Angi Holden 1996, first published here. **Julie Holder**: for 'A Begins Another' and 'Bun Stew', Copyright © Julie Holder 1996 first published here. **Michael Horovitz**: for 'Sea's Cape' from *Growing Up* (W. H. Allen). **David Kitchen**: for 'A Fistful of Pacifists', Copyright © Peter Bennett 1995, from *Never Play Leapfrog with a Unicorn* (Heinemann, 1995). **J Patrick Lewis**: for 'How to Tell a Camel', and 'Flamingo', Copyright © J Patrick Lewis 1990. **Candia McWilliam**: for 'Saints', first published in Angela Huth (ed): *Casting a Spell* (Orchard Books, 1991). **Sarah Matthews**: for 'Tyrannosaurus Rex' by

Stanley Cook, Copyright © Mrs K. M. Cook 1996, first published here. **Brian Merrick**: for 'Brother' and 'Sister', Copyright © Brian Merrick 1996, first published here. **Trevor Millum**: for 'Dennis Madge', Copyright © Trevor Millum 1996, first published here and for 'Trousers is a Silly Name', first published in *Poetry Express*, 1987. **Tony Mitton**: for 'Ten Things you Probably Never Thought to Ask About Elephants', Copyright © Tony Mitton 1996, first published here. **John Mole**: for 'The Mad Parrot's Countdown', Copyright © John Mole 1990 from *The Mad Parrot's Countdown* (Peterloo Poets, 1990). **Michaela Morgan**: for 'Writer's Workshop', Copyright © Michaela Morgan 1996, first published here. **Jenny Morris**: for 'Dodo', Copyright © Jenny Morris 1996, first published here. **Judith Nicholls**: for 'Riddle', Copyright © Judith Nicholls 1996, first published here. **David Orme**: for 'A Hard Life Without Ease', Copyright © David Orme 1996, first published here. **Jack Ousbey**: for 'Words', Copyright © Jack Ousbey 1996, first published here. **Penguin Books Ltd**: for 'Kite' by June Crebbin from *The Jungle Sale: Poems by June Crebbin* (Viking Kestrel, 1988), Copyright © June Crebbin 1988, and 'Fast Food' by Kit Wright from *Cat Among the Pigeons* (Viking Kestrel, 1987), text Copyright © Kit Wright, 1984, 1987. **The Peters Fraser & Dunlop Group Ltd**: for 'An Acrostic' by Roger McGough from *Nailing the Shadow* (Viking Kestrel), '40-Love' by Roger McGough from *After the Merrymaking* (Cape), and 'You Tell Me' by Michael Rosen from Michael Rosen and Roger McGough: *You Tell Me* (Viking Kestrel). **Louis Phillips**: for 'The Eraser Poem', Copyright © Louis Phillips, first published in Willard R. Espy (ed): *A Children's Almanac of Words at Play* (Hodder & Stoughton). **Gervase Phinn**: for 'It Takes One to Know One', Copyright © Gervase Phinn 1996, first published here. **Simon Pitt**: for 'At the End of School Assembly', Copyright © Simon Pitt 1996, first published here. **Janis Priestley**: for 'Terrible Lizard', Copyright © Janis Priestley 1996, first published here. **Random House UK Ltd**: for 'The ❩ and the full •' by Jez Alborough from *Shake Before Opening* (Red Fox). **Reed Consumer Books**: for 'My Snake' by Jack Prelutsky from *Something BIG has been Here* (Heinemann), Copyright © Jack Prelutsky 1989. **John Rice**: for 'Rhyme-osaur' and 'Baby Driver', Copyright © John Rice 1996, first published here. **Rogers Coleridge & White Ltd,** 20 Powis Mews, London W11 1JN: for 'Someone Stole The' by Brian Patten, from *Gargling with Jelly* (Viking, 1985) Copyright © Brian Patten 1985. **Scholastic Publications Ltd**: for 'Words in a Cage' by Geoffrey Summerfield from *Welcome and Other Poems* (1983). **Anne Serraillier**: for 'The New Weatherperson's First Appearance' by Ian Serraillier, Copyright © Anne Serraillier 1996, first published here. **Iain Crichton Smith:** for 'Incident', Copyright © Iain Crichton Smith 1996, first published here. **Ian Souter**: for 'The Word Is', and 'Can You?', Copyright © Ian Souter 1996, first published here. **Kaye Umansky** c/o Caroline Sheldon Literary Agency: for 'Chilly', Copyright © Kaye Umansky 1996, first published here. **Barrie Wade**: for 'Crack Another Yolk', Copyright © Barrie Wade 1995, from *Rainbow*, poems by Barrie Wade (OUP, 1995). **Dave Ward**: for 'Code Haiku', and 'Who Are You?', Copyright © Dave Ward 1996, first published here. **Colin West**: for 'An Angry Alligator' from *Casting a Spell* (Orchard Books, 1991), 'Jelly and Melons' from *Not To Be Taken Seriously* (Hutchinson, 1982), and 'Passers-by' from *What Would You Do With a Wobble-Dee-Woo?* (Hutchinson, 1988), all Copyright © Colin West. **David Whitehead**: for 'Doctor Spooner's Country Walk' and 'Leopard', Copyright © David Whitehead 1996, first published here. **G. M. Wilson**: for 'Ghost' by Raymond Wilson, Copyright © G. M. Wilson 1996, first published here.

Although every effort has been made to trace and contact copyright holders before publication, this has not been possible in a few cases. If notified, we will be pleased to rectify any errors or omissions at the earliest opportunity.